Contents

£6.99

Published by Pedigree Books Limited
Beech Hill House, Walnut Gardens, Exeter, Devon EX4 4DH.
E-mail books@pedigreebooks.co.uk
Published 2005
© Chapman Entertainment Limited 2005.
Licensed by Target Entertainment.

Welcome To Flowertot Garden

Hello, everyone!

I'm Fifi Forget-Me-Not and I live in Forget-Me-Not Cottage. I always have lots of gardening jobs to do and today I'm going to plant flowers in pots for my window boxes. Flowertot Garden is a very exciting place, there's always something happening here. You can soon read about some of my adventures and there are puzzles and games for you to enjoy, too. Have fun! Oh, fiddly flowerpetals! I almost forgot to tell you about my friends! Come and meet them...

Bumble™

Have you ever met a bee who gets hay fever? My friend Bumble does, so he sneezes quite a lot. He's also a very helpful bee and whenever he comes to see me, he always brings a present. I love his homemade honey flapjacks!

Mo™

Whenever I need to get across Flowertot Garden quickly, I go on Mo the mower. He's very fast and his trailer comes in useful for all sorts of things. He only ever says 'Brrrrm!' or 'Vrooom!' but we always know what he means!

Violet™

You could call this friend of mine Shrinking Violet, as she is the youngest of us Flowertots and a little bit shy. She is good at art and is always painting or making jewellery. She lives with Primrose in Flowertot Cottage.

Webby™

Wise old spider Webby always has an answer to any problem in the garden. She knows everything and we all go to her for advice. The only time she gets cross is when her web won't stay sticky and all her things fall off it!

Primrose™

You won't ever catch Primrose helping out in the garden – she hates getting dirty! She always likes to look her best and makes all her own pretty clothes. She keeps telling me that I should try wearing a dress, but I'm not so sure!

Pip™

Someone who does like to help in the garden is Pip Gooseberry. He loves to explore it, too, and can spend a whole afternoon roaming around on his scooter. He'll believe anything, though, which sometimes gets him into trouble!

Stingo™

There is a naughty wasp who spies on us from high up in Apple Tree House: this is Stingo, the garden pest.
He's always hatching harebrained plan after scatterbrained scheme and makes poor Slugsy help him.

Poppy™

This friendly Flowertot runs the market stall, selling all kinds of fresh, crunchy vegetables and juicy, sweet fruit. Poppy sells other things, too, which means that she is the one I rush to if I've forgotten a special ingredient!

Slugsy™

Stingo's slimy friend is almost as naughty, but he does have a soft centre and is especially fond of Primrose. He's much slower than his 'boss' and often has trouble keeping up. He's a singing slug, too!

Bumble Helps Out

Fifi Forget-Me-Not was busy in Flowertot Garden. She wanted to plant some flowers in pots for her window boxes before she went to have afternoon tea with her friends. "I've got so much to do before I go," she said to herself, hurriedly filling a pot with compost.

Fifi heard a buzz-buzzing above her and looked up. It was her friend, Bumble. She smiled as he flew down and landed clumsily with one of his legs in her bucket. "Oops! Hi, Fifi," he said, taking a jar from his bag. "I've brought you some of my special honey."

"Ooh, lovely. Thanks," said Fifi, taking the honey. "What are you doing?" asked Bumble. "I need to plant these flowers before I go to Violet and Primrose's house," replied Fifi. "I've planted myself," chuckled Bumble, as Fifi helped him out of the bucket.

Bumble offered to help Fifi and so she let him fill the flowerpots with compost for her. Fifi was so busy planting flowers that she did not realise the time until Bumble asked her when she was going for tea. "Fiddly flowerpetals!" she cried. "I'm late!"

Fifi rushed over to Mo and clambered aboard. "I have to go!" she called, starting up Mo's engine and racing off. "See you later!" Bumble gazed after her, then looked at the flowers that still needed planting: he would plant them himself, as a nice surprise for Fifi!

Violet and Primrose were wondering where Fifi was when there was a knock at the door. Primrose opened it. "Hello, Primrose. Hello, Violet," smiled Fifi. "Sorry I'm late, I've been planting flowers. "So we can see," sniffed Primrose, looking Fifi up and down.

"Come in," Violet said warmly. "Are those daisies for me? Thank you, Fifi. Come and sit down." Fifi was about to do as she was told, but Primrose stopped her. "Wait!" she cried, running out to fetch a leaf and putting it on the sofa. "Don't get anything dirty!"

Violet poured out dandelion tea for them all. "Would you like some honey in it?" she asked Fifi, holding out a jar. Just as Fifi was about to get some, the jar slipped out of Violet's hand and somersaulted to the floor. "Oh, Violet!" scolded Primrose.

All the honey spilled out of the jar. "What a mess!" scowled Primrose, peering at the golden puddle on the floor. "We can't have afternoon tea without honey!" wailed Violet. Fifi shrugged. "I have some that Bumble brought me, I'll go and get it," she said.

Bumble, meanwhile, had been busy planting Fifi's flowers for her. He had only one left to do. "Oh, wiggly worms!" he muttered, seeing the compost bucket empty. "There's no compost left! I shall just have to go to the compost heap and get some more."

"Bouncing buttercups!" Bumble gasped, when he reached the compost heap. "What a lot of compost!" He flew to the top and stood in the compost up to his ankles. When he had filled his bucket, he flapped his wings. Nothing happened: Bumble was stuck!

Fifi jumped back on to Mo and raced home. She parked by her flowerbed, then gasped at what she saw. "Look at this mess!" she said to herself. "What could have happened?" Then she heard a cry: "He-e-e-elp!" "That sounds like Bumble!" she exclaimed.

Fifi soon found her friend. "Oh, Bumble," she giggled, climbing up to him. She pulled on his legs until he came free, sending them both tumbling down the compost heap. "Thanks, Fifi," he giggled. "I thought I would never see a honey sandwich again!"

Fifi and Bumble went back to the flowerbed and cleared up the mess. Fifi taught Bumble how to plant a flower so they could plant them all again together. "We'll make a gardener of you yet, Bumble," giggled Fifi. "Ahem!" came Primrose's voice behind her.

"Fiddly flowerpetals!" cried Fifi, jumping up. "Fifi Forget-Me-Not FORGOT!" laughed her friends. "Sorry," said Fifi. "Let's have afternoon tea here – I have some blackberry pie!" "All right," agreed Violet. "As long as you don't forget the honey!"

Garden Chaos

Bumble has been having fun and hidden lots of Fifi's belongings in the Flowertot garden. See if you can help Fifi find her things. Each time you find something colour in the flower next to the item.

I love my Flowertot Garden

Webby

I love my garden, it's a special place to me.
Everyday is so much fun, it's where I love to be.

As the sun shines down I dust and clean, make things sparkle, shine and gleam.
I love my Flowertot garden, I love my Flowertot garden.

Pretty flowers, butterflies; sunshine in bright blue skies,
I love my Flowertot garden, I love my Flowertot garden.

Bumble

I love my garden, it's a special place to me.
Everyday is so much fun, it's where I love to be.

Eating honey's much more fun when you share it with someone.
I love my Flowertot garden, I love my Flowertot garden.

I love my garden, it's a special place to me.
Everyday is so much fun, it's where I love to be.

Pretty flowers, butterflies; sunshine in bright blue skies,
I love my Flowertot garden, I love my Flowertot garden.

Poppy

I love my garden, it's a special place to me.
Everyday is so much fun, it's where I love to be.

I'm layin' potatoes on my stall, not too high in case they fall
I love my Flowertot garden, I love my Flowertot garden.

I love my garden, it's a special place to me.
Everyday is so much fun, it's where I love to be.

I'm layin' potatoes on my stall, not too high in case they fall
I love my Flowertot garden, I love my Flowertot garden.

Primrose and Violet

I love my garden, it's a special place to me.
Everyday is so much fun, it's where I love to be.

Pretty flowers, butterflies; sunshine in bright blue skies,
I love my Flowertot garden, I love my Flowertot garden.

Fifi

I love my garden, it's a special place to me.
Everyday is so much fun, it's where I love to be.

As the sun shines down it's time for me, to get some carrots for my tea.
I love my Flowertot garden, I love my Flowertot garden.

Webby

I love my garden, it's a special place to me.
Everyday is so much fun, it's where I love to be.

As the sun shines down I dust and clean, make things sparkle, shine and gleam.
I love my Flowertot garden, I love my Flowertot garden.

I love my garden, it's a special place to me.
Everyday is so much fun, it's where I love to be.

Pretty flowers, butterflies; sunshine in bright blue skies,
I love my Flowertot garden, I love my Flowertot garden.

All

I love my garden, it's a special place to me.
Everyday is so much fun, it's where I love to be.

Pretty flowers, butterflies; sunshine in bright blue skies,
I love my Flowertot garden, I love my Flowertot garden.

Fifi's Chocolate Surprise

Fifi was busy blowing bubbles in her juice one morning when Pip Gooseberry and Bumble came bounding into her cottage kitchen.

"Hello, Pip! Hello, Bumble!" she smiled, taking the straw out of her mouth.

"Hello, Fifi," said Pip. "What are we going to do today?"

Fifi thought for a moment. Bumble and Pip waited eagerly to see what they could help with.

"We have to water plants, dig compost, make a...oh, fiddly flowerpetals!" Fifi struggled to think of the word. "What's it called?"

"Fifi Forget-Me-Not FORGOT!" chuckled Bumble and Pip.

Fifi tried to describe what she meant: "It's something that you eat and it's big and round."
"A lollipop!" guessed Pip.
"No," Fifi shook her head thoughtfully. "It's got cream inside and icing on top."
"A yummy biscuit?" said Bumble brightly.
"No, you make it for your friends," Fifi explained. "A...a...of course! A cake! I promised to make a chocolate cake for today's Flowertot tea party. I'd better get started! Now, where's that chocolate...?"
 "But what about all the gardening jobs?" asked Pip, disappointed. Fifi said that he could be in charge of the garden while she made the cake, so he skipped off happily to be the garden guard.

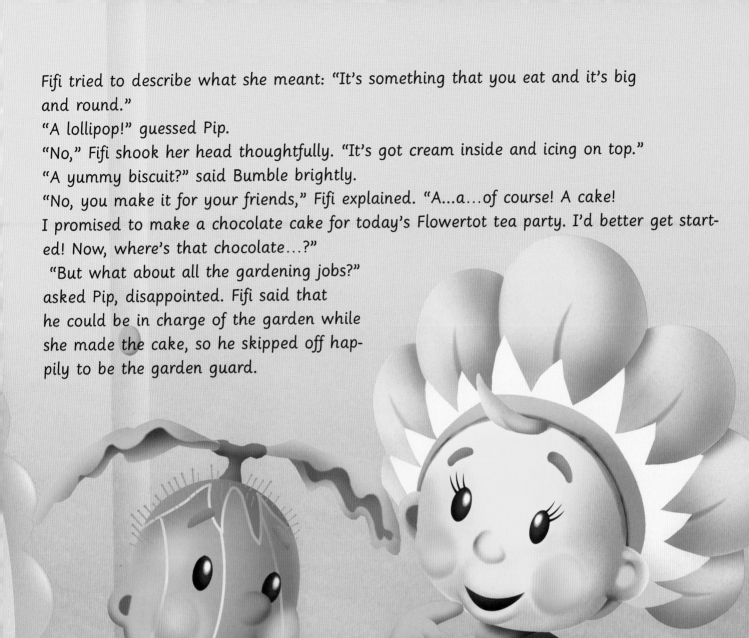

Fifi broke the chocolate into a bowl over a pan of hot water. She explained to Bumble that she was melting it to make the chocolate icing.

"Mmm," said Bumble, sniffing the warm chocolate. "That smells lovely!"

It wasn't long before the smell reached Stingo's Apple Tree House.

"What's that?" he said, scrambling along a branch and peering through his eyeglass. He looked across Flowertot Garden and his eyeglass rested on Fifi's open kitchen window.

"Bingo Stingo!" he exclaimed. "I spy chocolate! Jump to it, Slugsy!"

"Yessir!" Slugsy saluted his master and struggled to keep up with him as he raced towards Forget-Me-Not Cottage.

24

While the chocolate was melting, Fifi mixed some butter and sugar together in a bowl. Bumble put the flour on the table for her, but she needed some eggs first. "Oh, no!" she said, peering into the fridge. "I've run out of eggs! Come on, Bumble. We'll have to go to Flowertot Market and get some."
Fifi and Bumble hopped on to Mo and zoomed towards the market.
"Look after my melted chocolate, Pip!" Fifi shouted above the brrrrm brrrrrm of Mo's engine.
"I left it in the kitchen."
"Okay, Fifi!" Pip called back with a wave.

Once Fifi had gone, Stingo and Slugsy
sneaked past Pip and up to the cottage
door. Slugsy was not sure that they
should open the door without Fifi
inviting them in.

"Oh, slug of very little brain," sighed
Stingo. "Fifi's not here to ask us in.
Come on."

"Ooh, Fifi will be crosss with us,"
said Slugsy, following Stingo into the
kitchen. Stingo stood on the table
and looked around, but could not see
any chocolate.

"I bet Fifi's hidden it," he said, jumping
down. "But I've got a nose for
chocolate." He sniffed around the
kitchen until he found it.

"Hah hah! Bingo Stingo!" he exclaimed.

Stingo leaned over the bowl and breathed in the sweet smell. He stuck his long, curly tongue into it and slurped up some of the gooey chocolate.

"Mmm," he said, smacking his lips. "Delicious!"

"Can I have sssome, bosss?" Slugsy asked, hopefully.

"When we get home," snapped Stingo. "We've got to get this chocolate out of here before Fifi gets back."

Stingo picked up the bowl, just as Pip skipped through the door.

"I've got to look after Fifi's chocolate," Pip was saying to himself. He stopped and stared at Stingo and Slugsy.

"What are you doing?" he asked them.

"We were just talking about that elephant in the pond," said Stingo, carefully putting the bowl down again and nudging Slugsy. "Weren't we, Slugsy?"

"Ow! Um, yesss, the elephant, yesss we were," Slugsy stuttered.

"An elephant?" echoed Pip, wide-eyed. "Is there really an elephant in the pond?"

"Yes, it's been there ages," sniffed Stingo. "You'd better hurry if you want to see it."

"Wow!" said Pip, rushing out to find the elephant. Stingo took the bowl outside and tried to take off. "Phew!" he panted, after flapping his wings and getting nowhere.

"This bowl's too heavy!" Slugsy found a basket and poured the melted chocolate into it.

"See you back at the house," said Stingo, taking off with the basket.
"Aww, that'sss not fair!" wailed Slugsy. "You'll get there firssst and eat it all!"
Stingo cackled as he flew away, leaving Slugsy to make his own slow way home.

Stingo soon got tired of carrying the heavy basket. He slumped down at the
bottom of a hillock and waited. When Slugsy caught up, Stingo gave
him the basket.
"You pull and I'll push," he growled. Slugsy did as he was told and
Stingo pushed the basket with his head. Suddenly, the handle
broke and the basket tipped up, emptying chocolate all
over Stingo.
"Oh, no!" wailed Slugsy.

Slugsy stared at his chocolate-covered friend, then his eyes lit up.

"I can lick all that chocolate off," he drooled. After a few moments of slurping, Slugsy heard the sound of Mo's engine coming nearer and gulped.

"What have you done with my chocolate, Slugsy?" asked Fifi, jumping off Mo. "Poor Pip is very upset. He thinks it's his fault."

"Er, Stingo gave it to me, Fifi," Slugsy replied, a little ashamed.

"Oh! A chocolate wasp!" smiled Fifi, seeing Stingo on the grass. "That's very clever, Slugsy. I think I'll take it home for tea."

"B-b-but…" Slugsy began.

"M-m-mmph!" Stingo tried to complain through the setting chocolate.

It was time for afternoon tea. Fifi served slices of her cake to Violet, Pip, Primrose and Bumble.

"Haven't you forgotten something, Fifi?" sniffed Primrose, looking at her plain sponge cake.

"I don't think so, Primrose," smiled Fifi.

"You said you were making a chocolate cake," said Violet.

"Oh, the chocolate's here," chuckled Fifi, cracking the chocolate on Stingo's head with a teaspoon and breaking off a piece.

"That took you long enough!" Stingo buzzed furiously, wriggling out of his chocolate coating.

"Oh, hello Stingo!" Fifi teased. "Would you like some chocolate?"

Stingo scowled as everyone laughed. He strode to the door to fly off and buzzed crossly:

"Grr! I hate chocolate!"

A Marvellous Market Stall

Fifi has gone to Poppy's market stall to get some eggs for her cake.
Look at all the tasty fruit and vegetables Poppy is also selling!

Use your crayons or pens to colour in this picture of Fifi and Poppy. See if you can match the colours to those on the opposite page.

Cake Mix

Fifi's chocolate has mysteriously disappeared. Do you remember where it went? Now she will have to make a plain sponge cake! Use your pencil to practise writing the names of the ingredients she will use.

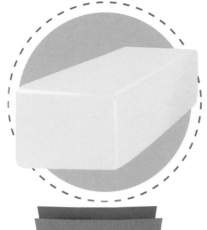

butter

butter

sugar

sugar

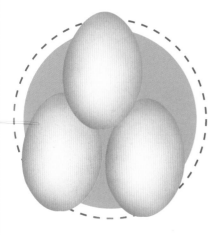

eggs

eggs

flour

flour

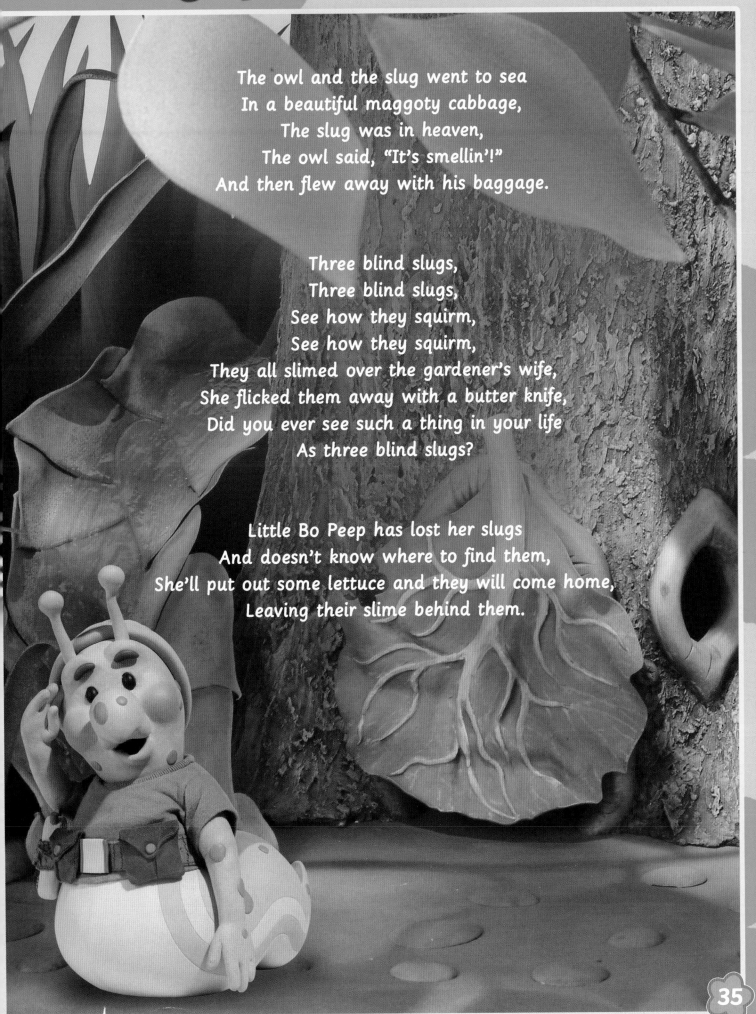

Slugsy's Rhyme Time

The owl and the slug went to sea
In a beautiful maggoty cabbage,
The slug was in heaven,
The owl said, "It's smellin'!"
And then flew away with his baggage.

Three blind slugs,
Three blind slugs,
See how they squirm,
See how they squirm,
They all slimed over the gardener's wife,
She flicked them away with a butter knife,
Did you ever see such a thing in your life
As three blind slugs?

Little Bo Peep has lost her slugs
And doesn't know where to find them,
She'll put out some lettuce and they will come home,
Leaving their slime behind them.

Stingo Gets Stuck

Bumble was taking some of his yummy honey flapjacks to Fifi Forget-Me-Not's. As he reached her cottage, he was almost lost in a cloud of dust. "Hello, Bumble!" Fifi called. "I'm just giving Mo a spring clean. He's very dusty!" "So I see," coughed Bumble.

Bumble helped Fifi to put the things back in Mo's clean trailer, then offered her a honey flapjack. "Mm, lovely," smiled Fifi, taking the tin from him. She tried to open it, but it was stuck fast. "Oh, dear," said Bumble. "Maybe there's some honey on the lid."

Bumble could not open the tin either, so he and Fifi went to see if Webby could help. "I'm sorry about the mess," she said, as she tried to take the lid off. "A huge cloud of dust came from nowhere and unstickied my web!" "Dust?" echoed Fifi. "Ah, um..."

"I'll see if Poppy's got something we can borrow," Webby interrupted, walking off along her web. "Ooh, yes," Fifi nodded, "and while you're gone, we'll clean your web. By the time you get back, it will be all sticky again!" "Thanks, Fifi!" smiled Webby.

Fifi and Bumble grabbed some dusters and set about cleaning Webby's web. Stingo had seen them arrive and came to find out what they were doing. "Bingo Stingo! I spy cake!" he whispered, spotting the tin. He crept towards it, licking his lips.

"Boss, mind that..." Slugsy began, but it was too late. CRASH! Stingo tripped over one of Webby's pans and landed with it on his head. "Oh, hello Stingo," said Fifi. "Have you come to help us clean Webby's web?" "Um, yes, of course," Stingo replied.

Stingo took off his pan hat. "We need to make it sticky again," Bumble explained. "I have a special tool," said Stingo, taking a whisk from his belt. "Do we have something sticky?" Bumble found a jar of honey and Stingo spun the whisk inside it. SPLAT!

"Whoah, Stingo! Turn it off!" cried Fifi, dodging the honey shower. Stingo tried, but the whisk seemed to be jammed. Suddenly, the whisk started to spin Stingo. "Slugsy, do something!" he spluttered. The others watched helplessly as he spun faster.

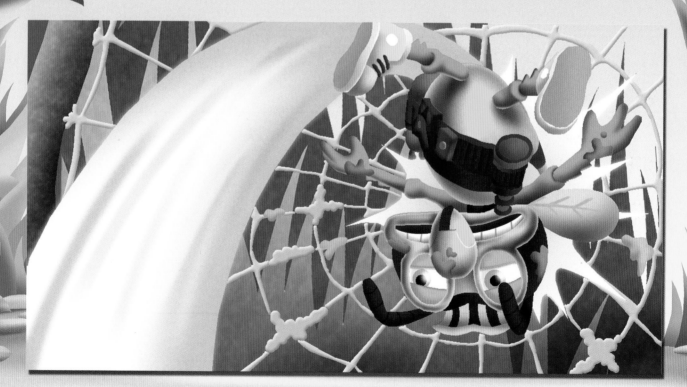

Stingo spun so fast that he flew through the air into the middle of Webby's web and hung there, upside down. "You were right, Stingo," said Slugsy, brightly. "It really works!" Stingo was not pleased. "Get me down from here!" he shouted, crossly.

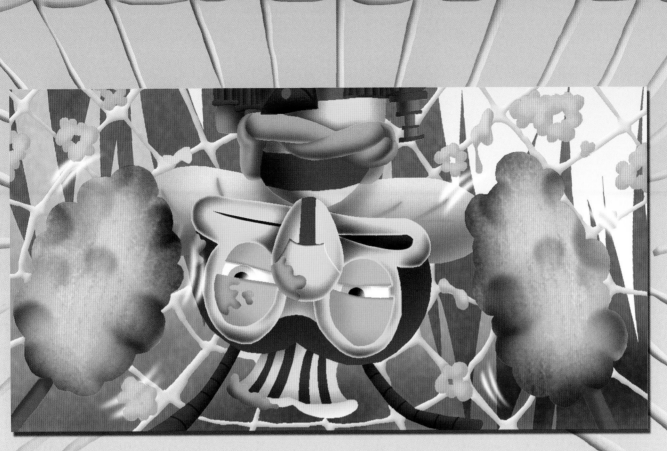

Fifi and Bumble tried to pull Stingo down from the web, but he was stuck fast. "I know," said Fifi. "Dust stopped the web being sticky...so if we clean the rest of the web, we can use the dust to unsticky Stingo!" Fifi, Bumble and Slugsy began to clean off the dust.

Once the web was clean, Fifi asked Bumble to help stick Webby's things back on to it. They were so busy that Stingo had to remind them he was there. "What about me?" he shouted. "Oops!" giggled Fifi. "Fifi Forget-Me-Not FORGOT!" smiled Bumble.

"This dust should unstick you in no time," said Fifi, rubbing Stingo with her dusty duster. "Ooh, ah! Careful, that tickles! Stop it!" giggled Stingo. "Just a bit more," said Bumble, joining in with his duster. "It's all right, boss," called Slugsy, "it's working!"

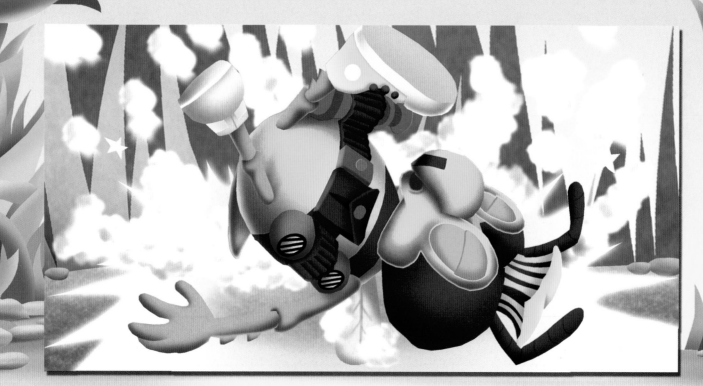

Little by little, Stingo came away from the web until BUMP! He dropped to the ground, sending up a little cloud of dust. "Stingo! What are you doing here?" asked Webby, arriving back with her lid opener. "Just hanging around," groaned Stingo.

Webby was pleased to see her web all clean and sticky again. "I expect you're hungry after all that hard work," she said, using the lid opener to get into the tin. POP! The lid flew off and everyone could see the honey flapjacks inside. "Mmm!" they all said.

"Thanks, Webby. Homemade honey flapjacks anyone?" Bumble asked proudly, handing them round. "Ooh, lovely," said Fifi and Webby, taking one. "What about me?" asked Stingo. "Stingo," laughed Fifi, "I think you've had enough honey for one day!"

Fifi's Shadow

Fifi has lost her shadow, help her find it by
matching Fifi with her missing shadow.

A

B

C

D

Answer: D

Bless You, Bumble!

Stingo has finally got one of Bumble's yummy honey flapjacks. He is really looking forward to it when...a-a-atchoo! Bumble's hay fever makes him sneeze all over it! Look at the two pictures and see if you can spot the five differences between them. The answers are at the bottom of the page.

Bumble: Eyes and braces button   Stingo: Wing, shoe and stripe

Bumble's Lost

Buttercups and daisies! Bumble is lost in Flowertot garden and needs Fifi to find him. Show Mo which way to go through Flowertot Garden so that Bumble can be free to fly again!

46

Hard at Work!

Stingo is enjoying the sunshine in Violet and Primrose's garden,
use your pens or crayons to copy the colours of the sunny scene
onto the picture at the bottom of the page.

Bouncing Blueberries

When Bumble went to see Fifi one morning, he arrived to find her putting some garden tools on to Mo's trailer.

"Hello, Bumble!" she smiled, climbing on to Mo. "Come on, we need to hurry."

Bumble joined his friend and they set off from Flowertot Garden. Fifi told him that they were going to work in Primrose's garden.

"But Primrose's garden is always so tidy," said Bumble with a puzzled frown.

"Blueberries, Bumble. Blueberries," Fifi said sternly. Bumble scratched his head and thought for a moment.

"Blueberries?" he repeated, as puzzled as ever.

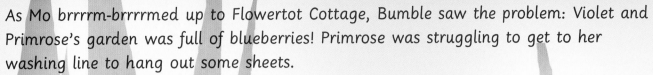

As Mo brrrrm-brrrrmed up to Flowertot Cottage, Bumble saw the problem: Violet and Primrose's garden was full of blueberries! Primrose was struggling to get to her washing line to hang out some sheets.

"Oh, what a mess!" she grumbled, tottering through the blueberries with her washing basket. She soon lost her balance and shrieked as she slipped over and found herself wrapped in sheets. Violet came to see if her friend was all right.

"I hate that blueberry bush," Primrose complained, snatching the sheets from her face. "It makes such a mess!"

"But they're such a beautiful colour," Violet said, stroking one of the blueberries.

"Blueberries are useless," Primrose grumbled, getting up. "No good for anything."
Violet offered to hang out the sheets. "Then I'll paint you a lovely picture to cheer you up," she smiled. "Look, here come Fifi and Bumble."
"Oh, Fifi, thank goodness you're here," said Primrose.
"We'll soon have your garden neat again, Primrose," smiled Fifi. "We'll have all these blueberries swept up in no time. All we need are our…oh, what are they? For sweeping…"
"Chimneys?" guessed Bumble.
"No, the things with lots of bristles," Fifi explained.
"Hedgehogs?" Bumble tried again.
"No. For cleaning up!"
"Brushes?" asked Violet.
"That's it!" said Fifi.
"Fifi Forget-Me-Not FORGOT!" everyone laughed.

Fifi and Bumble fetched their brushes from Mo's trailer. Primrose hurried off to do some shopping at Flowertot Market.

"Don't worry, Primrose," Fifi called after her. "Your garden will be all tidy by the time you come back."

Violet went inside to paint a picture for Primrose while Fifi and Bumble got to work. They took a broom each and tried to sweep the huge blueberries into a pile. Fifi puffed and panted as she swept three of them together. Bumble helpfully swept a blueberry towards Fifi's, but it scattered them like snooker balls.

"Oh, dear, this is no good," said Fifi.

Fifi and Bumble put their brooms down and tried to roll the blueberries together with their hands. However hard they tried, every time they rolled a blueberry up, another would roll away. One trundled towards the cottage door and Violet came out in time to see Fifi diving on it.

"Hello, Violet," giggled Fifi from the floor. "How's the picture going?"

"Not very well," Violet answered. "I've run out of paint."

"You can go and get some from my house if you like," said Fifi, standing up.

"Thanks. Do you need some help?" asked Violet, watching Bumble hopelessly chasing blueberries to and fro.

"No, we're fine. Don't worry!" Fifi said, chirpily. "'Bye!"

Fifi decided they needed something to put the blueberries in.

"Let's put them in Mo's trailer," suggested Bumble.

"Brilliant, Bumble!" smiled Fifi. She picked up a blueberry, but had only taken two steps when she stumbled and dropped it. To her surprise, the blueberry bounced away.

"Bouncing blueberries!" giggled Bumble.

Fifi scrambled to the blueberry, picked it up and bounced it away again.

"We can bounce the blueberries into the trailer, Bumble," she grinned, sitting on one and bobbing up and down on it. "Look!" Fifi moved her legs and sat on the blueberry as if it were a space hopper. She bounced around the garden on it and giggled.

"This is fun!" she called to Bumble, as she bounced the blueberry to the trailer and lifted it on. Bumble clambered on to the nearest blueberry and did the same. Fifi climbed on to another one and boing-boinged along.

"Wheeee!" she sang. "I can go really high!"

"So can I!" chuckled Bumble. He bounced on the blueberry as hard as he could. Boing, boing, SPLAT! His blueberry burst, squirting purple juice all over Fifi.

"Uh-oh!" said Bumble, sitting up on his flattened berry and looking at the mess.
"Sorry, Fifi!"
Fifi licked the juice that was running down her face.
"Yum! Bouncing, bursting blueberries!" she smiled.

Fifi bounced hard on her blueberry until SPLAT! It burst all over Bumble.

"Fifi! Mm, you're right," Bumble giggled. "That juice is yummy!" He ran to burst another berry over Fifi, then she did yet another over him. They laughed as they took turns to burst the berries and catch the delicious juice in their mouths until they tired themselves out. As they lay, giggling, amongst the burst blueberries, Bumble's face fell.

"Fifi, look at the mess we've made!" he said. Fifi looked round and stopped giggling.

"There's juice on Primrose's sheets!" she gasped.

They tried to wipe the juice off with a leaf, but only added green stains to the purple splodges.

"Fifi! Bumble!" Violet was back and hurried over to them. "What have you done? Those sheets are ruined!"

"And the garden's messier than ever," Bumble added, ashamed of himself.

"And I haven't done my painting," said Violet. "There are only seeds in your paint box, Fifi!"

"This garden looks like an exploded paint box," sighed Fifi. "Diddly dandelions! That's given me an idea!" She grabbed one of Violet's paintbrushes and stuck it in some of the blueberry juice. "Maybe you can do a picture for Primrose after all."

Primrose looked from the paintbrush to the blueberries to the sheets and her face brightened.

"Fabric paints!" she exclaimed.

Violet used strokes of her brush to transform
the splodges and stains into flowers and leaves, while Fifi and Bumble raced to clear up the garden.

"Surprise!" they all shouted when Primrose returned. They waited nervously as she looked at her newly painted sheets.

"They're a bit purple," she began, "almost blueberry colour…"

"Let's see what they look like in your room!" suggested Violet, carrying them inside for her. Fifi and Bumble waited until at last, Primrose came out, waving two pillowcases.

"They look perfect!" she beamed. "Violet's going to do some pillowcases to match!"

"Well done, Violet," Fifi smiled, with a wink. "Where would we be without you?"

A Bouncing Blueberry Race

Bouncing blueberries! Violet and Primrose's garden is full of blueberries so Fifi and Bumble have come to help clear it. They are going to bounce the blueberries to Mo's trailer.

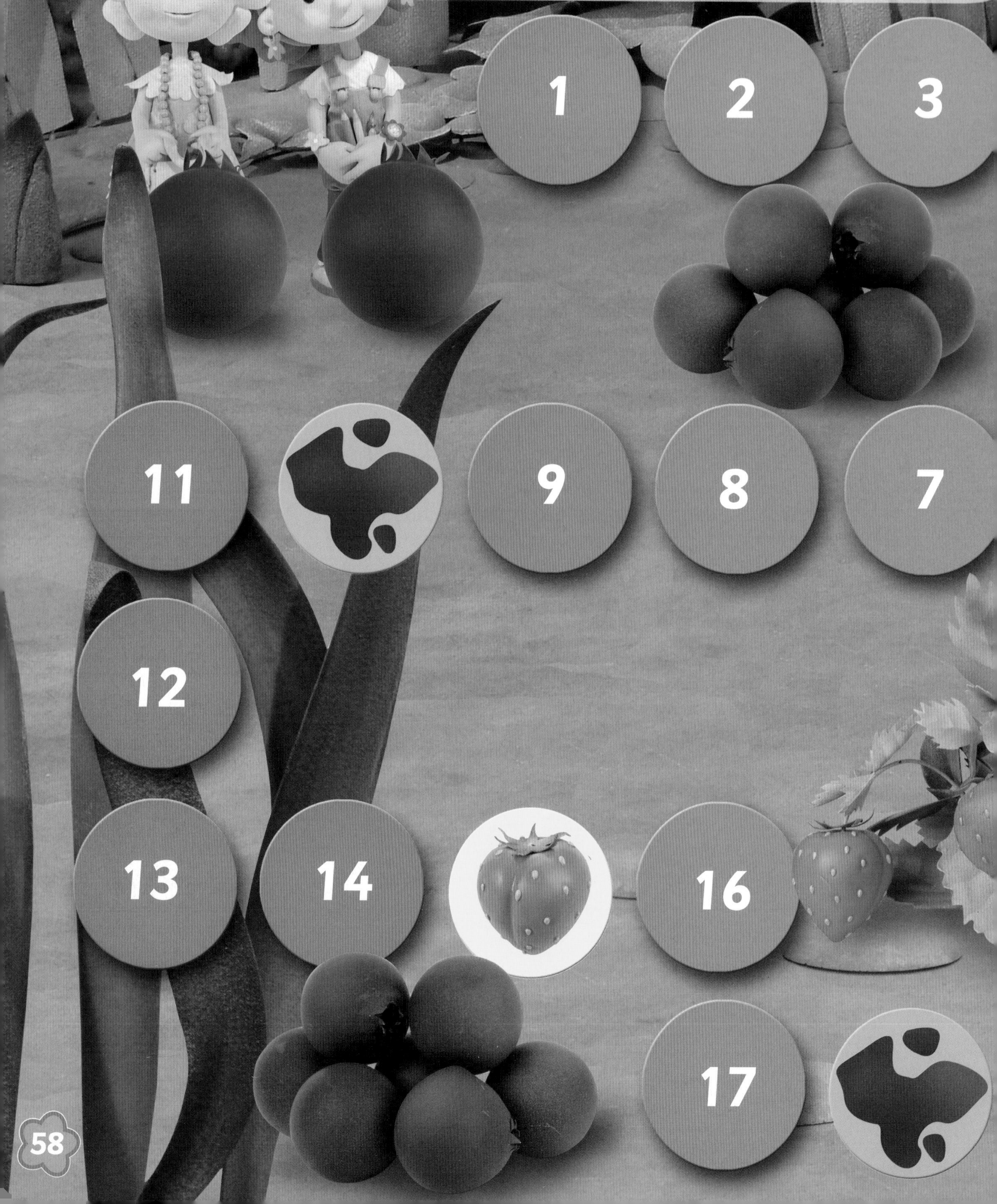

1 2 3

11 9 8 7

12

13 14 16

17

You and a friend can jump on a blueberry and bounce with them if you can find a dice and two counters.
Place your counters on the start. Take turns to throw the dice and work your way round the garden, making sure you throw a six to start. If you land on a strawberry, you can bounce on two spaces. If you land on a burst blueberry, you must miss a go to get on another one! The first one to get their blueberry to Mo is the winner. Bounce away!

4

26

27

5

25

29

24

30

22

31

21

19   20

Yummy Berry Juice

Bumble loved the juice from the bursting blueberries! Join the dots to see what sort of berry juice he is slurping now, then use your pens or crayons to colour the picture. What other sorts of berry can you think of?

Slugsy Loves Primrose

You are a lovely Flowertot
In fact, I like you...a lot!
I'm just a slug and full of slime
But Primrose, you always look divine!

Thank you, Slugsy, for your rhyme,
But you are, as you say, just full of slime,
I am divine and could never hug
A creepy, crawly, slimy slug!